$\mathcal{S}$weet 21 $\mathcal{B}$irthday $\mathcal{B}$all

Sometimes Love Really Can Wait

J. Adams

J. Adams

Jewel of the West Publishing

ISBN-13: 978-0615608259

ISBN-10: 0615608256

Library of Congress Control Number: 2012903618

To Marcia Lynn McClure

You said I could do it and I did!

I'm grateful for your friendship.

Thanks for being the loudest voice in the cheering section!

Every step I have taken in this life, every path I have chosen, every moment of laughter, of tears, of triumph and trials, every single road has led me to this one moment. A moment of pure bliss and happiness.

And I know now with absolute certainty, I am that I might have joy.

Dominique's Diary

Venice, Italy

Running down the flooded walkways of Venice, Marcello Giannini weaves his way through the passing tourists, making it to the San Marco *piazza* just in time to catch the train to Treviso. He'd decided against picking his car up from the garage and driving to his parent's home, opting to take the train instead. He has no plans to drive for the next few days. Besides, he can use his father's car if he really needs to.

By the time Marcello makes it to a seat, his hair is plastered to his brow. Combing his fingers back through the wet black waves, he smiles, looking forward to his mother's cooking. At twenty-two years old and the owner of one of Venice's most popular pastry shops, Marcello isn't rich, but his lifestyle is a comfortable one. He lives simply and has all he needs.

"Except a wife," he can hear Mama saying, a phrase that is repeated each time he comes home. He is sure he will hear it again during this visit as well.

Yesterday his mother informed him that they would be having guests. A friend and business acquaintance of his father's is visiting from the United States. Marcello has heard nothing but good things about this family and he is looking forward to meeting them.

***

"You're all wet," a small American voice calls to Marcello from one of the second floor windows as he approaches the door.

Looking up, he grins. "That I am," he responds in English. "Do you think it will be all right for me to come in and dry off?"

"I suppose," she answers. "Just wipe your feet off really good first, okay?"

Marcello chuckles. "Okay."

"Ciao, Marcello," his mother greets him, kissing both cheeks. "You are all wet."

"Yes, I have been told this," he says, a grin splitting

his face as his little informant approaches. "And who is this beautiful little angel who so dutifully suggested that I wipe my feet thoroughly before coming in?"

His mother laughs. "This little darling is Miss Dominique Jensen, one of our guests."

"It is a pleasure to meet you, Dominique." He bows royally, drawing a giggle from the little girl. Taking in the fair tone of the child's skin and the glorious head of black curly ringlets, Dominique reminds him of a doll on display in the window of one of the city gift shops. He knows the girl is the product of mixed race parents, her mother being black and her father white, and though he has yet to meet them, he can clearly see the ethnicity of both in their daughter.

Marcello drops to one knee and asks, "How old are you?" musing that she is getting an early start in female bossiness.

"I'm eight. How old are *you*?"

He laughs. Leaning toward her he whispers, "I'm twenty-two, but don't tell anyone, okay? Mama keeps bugging me about getting married."

She moves closer and whispers back, "You want me to talk to her?" and Marcello bites his lip, stifling his laughter.

"Maybe later. Shall we go and meet your parents?"

"Sure," she says, grabbing his hand. "Come on."

***

For the next few days, Marcello and Dominique are inseparable. No matter what he is doing or where he's going, the little girl's hand is always tucked in his and he is helplessly twisted around her little finger.

From a game of checkers in front of the living room fireplace to playing with Dominique's dolls in a mini pink tent on the covered patio, to chasing one another through the Giannini's olive grove, watching animated movies with a bowl of popcorn between them, and finally, Marcello carrying the sleeping little girl up and tucking her in when she can no longer keep her eyes open. Every moment is full.

Marcello extends his stay and fills the time taking Dominique and her parents picnicking, shopping and sightseeing. He and Dominique spend an afternoon baking cookies and little cakes, and then have a tea party afterward. A couple of stuffed bears and a few dolls are in attendance.

Marcello enjoys every moment he spends with

Dominique. He completely adores the little girl and now refers to her as *mi* Domi.

***

Saying goodbye to Dominique at the airport is one of the hardest things Marcello has ever done. Dropping to his knees, he tearfully hugs her and she clings tightly to him, crying against his neck.

"Shhh, don't cry" he whispers. "I will come and see you in the States when summer comes."

"You promise?" she asks between sobs. "Promise to come, Cello."

He smiles at her endearing nickname for him. "I promise, *mi* Domi. I promise."

"And you can't get married cause your wife won't let you come."

Marcello meets Evan and Serena Jensen's smiles over Dominique's shoulder. "Don't worry, baby girl," he whispers against her ear. "I'm waiting for you to grow up."

Wiping his eyes, Marcello stands at the foot of the escalator and watches the family until they are no longer in sight. He vows then and there to never let a year pass without seeing his Domi. He had made this promise to her, not fully understanding that the hold she has on his heart is much bigger than them both.

***

I miss Cello. Can't wait til summer.

He promised to come.

He promised.

p.s. I'm gonna marry Cello when

I grow up.

Dominique's Diary

Denver, Colorado

Thirteen years later

Squinting in the bright sun, I take a pair of shades from my shirt pocket and slip them on. Today is another scorcher and even the straw hat I've worn through the summer doesn't seem to help. We've been out in the sun for a while, weeding the small flowerbeds behind the rest home and I worry about the residents overheating. But we seem to have gotten a lot done so I decide to call it a day and quickly begin ushering everyone back inside.

For the past two years I've volunteered once a week at Shady Oaks, helping out in any way I can and I've enjoyed it immensely. Except for a few cranky residents, the elderly people living here are very sweet and loving, and I appreciate the time I get to spend with them, especially the women. Even in their dependent state, these grandmothers and great-grandmothers are still full of fun and they sincerely enjoy life. In fact, they enjoy it so much, the staff has decided to have a costume ball for the residents. The elderly group went on a shopping trip this past weekend, and all week long the women have been telling me about the costumes they chose. And they insist that I attend. Not only do they want me here to help them get ready, they've decided that I need to add some "snazzy pzazz" to my life.

The women wonder why I don't have a boyfriend and constantly offer to fix me up with grandsons, great-grandsons, and any other unattached guy they can think of. They've even tried their matchmaking skills on me and the two single men on the staff. They are definitely a fun and funny bunch of women.

Truthfully, I have been on exactly two dates in my life. The first was with a classmate when I was sixteen. The guy tried to kiss me the entire hour we were together. When he realized it just wasn't going to happen, he took me home and never asked me out again, which was no big loss as far as I was concerned. The second date was the winter I turned seventeen. I really didn't consider it a date since we were meeting up with a group to go bowling. We hadn't even pulled away from the curb when he suddenly turned into Mr. Octopus Hands. It was probably the shortest date in history–timed at exactly thirty seconds–long enough for me to get in and out of his car.

I haven't been out with anyone since. I've followed the dictates of my heart for as long as I can remember. And there-in lies my problem.

After making sure everyone is inside and the pastries I brought have been distributed, I leave and head home to my amazing job–the best job in the world.

Cake decorating.

I started decorating cakes for a living at sixteen. Marcello taught me. In fact, Marcello taught me everything about baking, giving me my first real lesson the summer I turned nine–the first time he kept his promise to come. Pulling into the driveway, I put the car in park and smile, allowing my thoughts to drift back to the day he came.

Twelve years ago.

The moment Marcello walks through the security gate I yell, "Cello!" and fly into his arms, clinging to his neck as he lifts me, spinning me around. "I've miss you, mi Domi," he says, kissing my cheek.

"You kept your promise," I say, touching his face.

"Always, angel." He smiles, kissing my other cheek.

As soon as he's finished greeting my parents with kisses and embraces, I take his hand and hold it tightly, never wanting to let go.

Marcello stays for two weeks, and many of these days are spent in the kitchen baking cookies and cakes. Mama's kitchen is a disaster area the first couple of times, thanks to me, but I get better at keeping the messes small and my batches of cookies begin to look and taste better. By the last day of Marcello's visit, my baking skills are improved substantially.

But my heart is breaking all over again. Today is my ninth birthday and he is leaving. This time I can't bear the ride to the airport, so I don't go. Again, I have to say goodbye to him, and again, I cling to him, unable to let him go.

"I will be back next summer, baby girl," he says as tears

trail down his cheeks.

"You promise?"

"I promise."

I hold his face in my hands. "And don't get married, okay? If a lady asks you, say no, cause you are mine, okay?"

He gives me a watery smile. "Always, **bella.** *Now, as soon as I am gone, go up and open the present I left on your dresser."*

Watching Daddy drive away with my Cello is just as painful as it was in Italy as the escalator took me farther from him. Wiping my face, I run up to my room and unwrap the small box. Inside is a silver charm bracelet. The largest of the charms is round and flat with a heart engraved on one side and an inscription on the other.

For mi Domi.

I promise. Always.

Your Cello

***

"Always," I whisper, drawing my thoughts back to the present, reverently fingering the bracelet on my wrist.

Always.

I don't know what that means anymore.

"My birthday is in two days."

Mama reaches across the kitchen table and squeezes my hand. "He will come, honey."

"I don't think he will this time. He's normally here by now. He should have called last week telling us when he would be here."

"Maybe you should call him."

"I can't, Mama."

"Why not?"

I release a painful sigh. "Because I don't want to hear that he is going to finally break his promise. I don't think I could bear it."

"Maybe he has a good reason."

I blink away the tears stinging my eyes. "I'm sure he does, but it would still be hard."

She pats my hand. "He will come." She picks up my invitation to the costume ball. "Did you find something to wear?"

I absently nod, my mind still immersed in thoughtful grief. "I found an Greek goddess outfit."

"Oooo, I bet you will look beautiful."

"It really doesn't matter since Marcello won't be here to see it. Maybe he's finally seeing someone and has a girlfriend. His last letter sounded that way."

"I don't know, honey, but I doubt it."

"Things can change, Mama. Meeting the right person can change everything. It *does* change everything."

"This is true, but only if it's really love. And if he has found someone, as one of his very best friends, you need to support him, even be happy for him."

"How can I, Mama? I would most likely never see him again, and I don't know if I would ever get over the loss."

"Honey, don't write him off. Marcello would never

do anything to hurt you. You have to trust in that."

"I'll try." Giving my mother a sad smile, I get up and seek the solace of my room.

Glancing at the framed print of Cinderella hanging on my wall, I think back to a time when I believed in fairy tales. It would be more realistic to believe in the original Grimm's tales, the way the Grimm brothers really wrote them. Italians have their own fairy tales, too. Marcello used to tell them to me. The first summer he came to visit, he read me the Italian tale of "The Three Sisters." I remember it well.

"Are you ready?" Marcello asks, sitting next to me on the patio glider swing.

I nod in anticipation. "Ready."

"You're sure you want to hear it? It's pretty grim."

"I'm sure, Cello. Now quit stalling and read."

"All right, Miss Bossy, here we go."

"There once was a woman who had three daughters; the two older daughters were very unlucky, but the youngest, Nella, was very fortunate. One day a prince married her and hid her from his wicked mother, visiting her in secret.

Whenever she threw a powder in a fire, he would come to her on a crystal road. Her sisters discovered this and broke the road, so that the prince was injured when he was coming to her. He was dying. His father proclaimed that whoever cured him would marry him if it was a woman, or have half the kingdom, if it was a man."

I interrupt the story, coming up with what I think is a brilliant idea. "If it was a woman, she could marry the prince and still have half of her father's kingdom."

"And how is that?" Marcello asks.

"Well, when he dies she could have it all anyway."

He laughs. "Well thought, Domi. Now let me finish."

> *"Nella heard the proclamation of the prince's father and set out. Hiding in a tree, she overheard an ogre tell his wife about the illness, and how only the fat from their bodies could cure the prince. She climbed down and presented herself at their door as a beggar. The ogre, greedy for her flesh, persuaded his wife to let her stay. When they slept, Nella killed them and took their fat. She brought it to the king and cured the prince. He said he could not marry her because*

he was married already; Nella asked if he wanted to be married to the person responsible, and the prince blamed her sisters. Nella then revealed herself as his wife and her sisters were thrown in an oven."

"That was it?" I ask, scrunching up my nose.

"Yes, that's it."

"Boy, Italian's don't get out much, do they?"

Marcello throws his head back and laughs. "Sorry, mi Domi. I will choose another story and try to do better next time."

***

I sigh. *No happily ever after. Like life.*

Deep down, a part of me still believes in a happily ever after because of the tiny bit of hope that continues to futilely hang on. No matter how much I tell myself it's pointless, that small hope will not leave me.

Pulling a decorated shoe box from beneath my bed, I open it and take out a stack of letters from Marcello. I've received exactly fifty letters over the years and I keep them all in the order he wrote them. Sitting in the middle of the bed, I read the very first letter he sent to me.

My Dearest Dominique,

Saying goodbye to you at the airport last week literally ripped my heart in two. I miss you so much already. The time we were able to spend together was the happiest week of my life, baby girl. Now, when I am not working, I'm so bored I don't know what to do because you kept me so busy. I have no one to play dolls with or chase through the olive grove, or bake little cakes and have tea parties with. That was my first tea party, you know? The one we shared with you and your doll, Mandy and your bears, Sid and Fred. We will have to have another one when I see you again.

It is raining again. I don't think I will ever walk in the rain without thinking of you, mi Domi.

I refold the letter and pull out another.

Thank you for the photos of us at the zoo and the children's museum. You are twelve now and growing up fast, and I wish I didn't have to miss so much of your life. You grow more beautiful every day. I have begun a scrapbook to keep our photos in (I know, me, scrap booking just boggles the mind) but it is getting pretty full already. I will need to start another soon.

It is fall here and we have started the olive harvest. As I help to spread the nets to catch the olives, I can't help but think of how much you would love this. Of course, knowing you, after working a few minutes, you would initiate an olive fight and there would be none left to press for oil. The visual makes me smile.

I miss you so, mi Domi.

And another.

I am so glad I could be there for your birthday. Mama mia, you're sixteen already! Time is passing so quickly. It seems like it was just yesterday when this beautiful little American girl stood in my parent's window and told me to wipe my feet well before coming in. I smile every time I think on that day. You were such a bossy little thing, which made you all the more adorable.

Have you been asked out on a date yet?

And at the top of the stack sits one that I received just two months ago.

You were right when you said I have changed, but so have you. I guess it was inevitable, right? Nothing ever stays the same. This is something we both know.

I am sorry I couldn't stay long enough to celebrate your twentieth birthday, but I hope you ate a big piece of cake for me. It was a masterpiece, if I do say so myself.

There is so much to say, so many important things I need to tell you, but I would rather say them face to face. I know my news will come as a surprise, but there is no one else I would rather share this with. We've always been there for one another and I hope that part won't ever change.

Reading his words again brings forth thoughts that are much too painful to linger on for even the smallest increment of time. I place the letter back in the box and slide it under the bed. Then, unable to hold back any longer, I press my face against the pillow and cry.

I have loved Marcello Giannini for as long as I can remember. At first it had just been a child's love, then a child's crush. By seventeen, it had grown into something entirely different–something achingly beautiful and painfully exquisite and tender. At seventeen the love of a child had vanished, and in its place was the heart of a woman–a heart tempered and refined with an emotion that nothing in this earthly sphere could rival. Nothing could rival it then, and nothing can now.

At seventeen I began to notice things about Marcello I hadn't before–the vividness of his blue eyes, the perfectness of his handsome face, the solidness of his six-feet-three-inch muscular form, the softness of his lips when he kissed my brow. I began to notice what just looking at him did to me. But with this new awareness had come reality, and that reality is I will always be too young. In a literal sense, I will always be his 'baby girl.' I'm about to lose what little of him I've always had, and there is nothing I can do about it.

But I understand now. My love for him was never a guarantee, and I must accept that he most likely will never be mine. I don't think he ever was.

**

Four years ago.

As I blow out the candles on the beautiful cake Marcello made for me, I can sense that something has changed. As usual, Marcello's visit is the highlight of my summer, but something is definitely different.

Our days are spent together with my parents and conversation flows easily, but when it is just Marcello and me, the exuberance that has always filled his eyes and is usually so tangible I could feel it, is not there. I begin to wonder if there is something wrong. I start to wonder if he not longer likes me and is tired of coming to visit. When I can no longer hold my anguish inside and I express to him my worry, tears immediately fill his eyes and he assures me that he could never tire of coming to see me. Touching my cheek, he tells me, "Mi Domi, you mean more to me than I can freely express."

The next three summers are amazing, bringing with them memories I will always treasure. Each experience is a snapshot taken by the camera that is my mind, permanently scrap-booked in a special section of my heart—a section where all things pertaining to Marcello are stored.

***

One year ago.

Marcello arrives a week before my birthday and leaves the day before. His only explanation is he is needed at the pastry shop. It takes every ounce of strength I possess to keep from bursting into tears and begging him to stay. Those days are long gone now. I am no longer a child and I will not allow myself to act like one, even though I am dying inside. Before going to the airport, he gives me a present. It is a gift basket of Godiva chocolates. Hanging from from a ribbon around one of the candy bars is another charm. It is a small silver heart. Marcello attaches it to the bracelet he gave me. There is also an excerpt from one of the works of Dante Alighieri, an Italian poet.

There is a gentle thought that often springs to life in me, because it speaks of you. Its reasoning about love's so sweet and true

His parting embrace is exquisitely tender and filled with a warmth I have never experience in his arms before. The repeated brush of his lips against my brow, the press of his wet cheek against mine, and the emotional groan that escapes him are all new to me. But his whispered, "Don't cry, baby girl," followed by, "I'll be back next summer, I promise," hasn't changed.

***

And he isn't here.

Drying my face, I get up and pull my costume from the closet. Marcello has always said yellow is my color. He would have liked this dress.

But I guess it doesn't matter anymore, does it?

Resigning myself to accept this, I will go to the rest home party and try to enjoy myself and make the most of it. After all, the ball is on my birthday. That is a reason to celebrate.

But deep down I know that even though I will be surrounded by a room full of people, I will still be alone.

"Happy Birthday to me," I whisper to my reflection. The Greek style gown fits me well, accentuating curves I never realized I had, but the yellow that normally cheers me up when I wear it has no effect on my growing sadness. Because my mascara is repeatedly smudged by the tears I can't seem to stop shedding, I again touch up my makeup using waterproof this time. Mama had helped with my hair, styling my thick locks in an up-do that actually looks stunning. I take one last moment to examine myself, futilely wishing yet again that my efforts were not such a waste.

Grabbing my sweater and purse, I head down and

load the beautiful cakes the rest home staff had ordered for tonight into my car. The two rectangle masterpieces, decorated with a garden of multicolored rosebuds are a work of art and are the most beautiful cakes I've ever done. I had taken extra time, wanting them to be perfect, because my elderly friends deserve the best. When it comes to baking, Marcello taught me to do nothing less. He taught me so many things . . .

***

When I arrive at the home, the party is in full swing. The decorations of balloons, snowflakes and mini Christmas lights are colorful, giving the large social hall a festive feel. And I am amazed at the diverse costumes. The residents are dressed in everything from the Tudor royals to pop stars to pioneers. One of the women is even dressed like a young Laura Ingalls, decked out in two braids. She is sitting behind a small table with a few books from the Little House series in front of her, like she is at a book signing. There are even a few staff members playing along by forming a little line in front of the table. It's totally hilarious.

However, I am a little puzzled that all the women

are dressed and hadn't needed my help after all. I guess the staff stepped in and took care of them.

George Gaines, one of our residents approaches me dressed like an eighty-year-old viking. "Lookin' good, George!"

"Thank you, Dominique. And I gotta say you are a babe! You look good enough to eat! I'd like to spread you on some toast and gobble you up!"

A blush quickly heats my cheeks and I'm sure my face is scarlet. "You're a smooth talker, George," I say, trying to cover my embarrassment.

"Don't I know it! Gotta stay sharp for the ladies." He flexes one of his small arms and I bit my lip to keep from laughing.

"Well, I will leave you to make the rounds and check out the other babes."

"Will do," he says with a grin and walks off.

Emily, one of our oldest residents, rolls by in her wheelchair dressed like Cleopatra.

"Make way!" she yells. "I'm looking for my Anthony! Anthony, my love, where art thou?" And this time, nothing can stop me from laughing.

"Wow!" I say as Angela, one of our nurses glides

over, dressed as a French maid. "What are you trying to do, send these old men into cardiac arrest?"

"Naw, these old guys are tough as nails. George and Sam have already pinched my rear end twice."

"Angela!"

"Ah, hell, I don't care. Besides, it was probably the best thrill they've had in years."

I laugh. "I'm sure they appreciate your thoughtfulness and concern for their well-being."

"I know, tell me about it!" She looks over my shoulder. "Hey, stop that, Hamilton! What are you pouring into that punch bowl?" I giggle as she runs off.

***

As the night wears on, a growing sadness comes over me again and I suddenly wish it was over. Dancing with the male residents (some of them with walkers–a challenging feat indeed) giggling like school girls with the women as they check out and discuss the men, and even leading a conga line hasn't kept my thoughts of Marcello at bay.

Walking over to one of the windows, I stare out at the half moon. It has become a habit for me ever since Marcello's last visit when we spent a few evenings sitting on the front porch steps holding hands, gazing up at the moon. We didn't say much. We were each lost in our own thoughts, and several times I wished I could know what he was thinking.

I wonder what he is thinking now.

I close my eyes and swallow back the rising emotion. I miss him so much. My heart literally aches for him, and my whole being is in agony. I love him, and I need him. And I know that won't ever change. For as long as I live, my soul will cry out for only him.

For a moment I think about my most recent letter to him.

A month ago.

Dear Marcello,

Just one month and you will be here! I can't wait to see you. I have missed you so much, more so this year than before. I guess I enjoyed your last visit so much, I didn't want it to end. Maybe that was because it was so short. Well, that's not the only reason, but I really hated saying goodbye, just like always. I think of you every day and I hope all is well with you and your family.

I miss you. Oops, I guess I already said that.

Yesterday, I took a friend's kids to the zoo and I couldn't help thinking of the summer you took me. Of all the times I had been to the zoo, and have gone since, the summer I went with you was the most memorable because you were here and we were together. Your visits have always been the highlight of my summer, of my entire year.

Summer has come early this year. The days are scorching hot, but the evenings are wonderful. I sit on the porch and stare up at the moon a lot, and each time I do, I imagine you here, looking up at it *with me. It makes not seeing you a little easier—not much, but some.*

Are you thinking of me, Cello? Do you think of me and remember?

My forehead is pressed against the cool glass and I am lost in my thoughts for some time. When I finally open my eyes, I glimpse a reflection in the window pane–a reflection of the face that is as familiar to me as my own. The social hall growing silent, I slowly turn and the whole room fades away.

"Happy Birthday, *Mi bella* Domi."

"Happy Birthday, Dominique!" the crowd suddenly repeats, then begins the birthday song.

It takes me a moment to grasp that he is really here. Dressed in a black suit and blue silk shirt, with hair perfectly tousled and ocean blue eyes that are again filled with exuberant wonder, Marcello is the most beautiful thing I have ever seen. I am still frozen in place, unable to move and my heart pounds harder with each step he takes toward me. I glance over his shoulder at my parents, huge grins splitting their faces. Mama had known all along, but she never gave anything away.

I can't believe it! This was all for me!

"But how . . ."

"I arranged it all last year."

Someone turns the music back up and the residents begin to dance again.

"I can't believe you're here," I breathe when he is standing before me, so close that I can feel his warmth, smell his cologne, see the tears in his smiling eyes–eyes that say so much. "I didn't think you would come." Unable to help myself, I wrap my arms around his neck and cling to him, tears streaming down my cheeks as his arms encircle me and tighten. How I have missed his embrace!

Holding me close, we slowly begin to dance to the soft music. Pressing his lips to my ear, he whispers, "I told you I would come."

I draw back a little to look into his eyes. "And you have always kept your promises."

He smiles. "Do you remember what I whispered to you the first time I told you goodbye at the airport in Venice, when you thought I would marry and not be able to come?"

I nod, but I am unable to voice to the words, afraid to believe them. I know he senses this.

"I said, "Don't worry, baby girl, I'm waiting for you to grow up."" He pauses, looking into my eyes. "I am hopelessly in love you, Dominique. I love you so much more than I can express to you in words."

"I'm in love with you, too, Marcello. I've always loved you."

Taking my hand, he leads me through the social hall doors out to the patio. Slipping his arms around my waist, he tightens his embrace and I relax with my back against his chest as we gaze up at the moon. I shiver at the feel of his lips against my ear.

"I've always loved you, Dominique. But until now, I wasn't free to. I was bound by age and couldn't speak the words, but, oh, how I longed to!"

Closing my eyes, I smile. "There has never been anyone for me but you, Marcello. I tried, but my heart could never open to anyone else."

He sighs. "*Mi bella* Domi, you claimed my heart the moment you spoke to me from my parent's window. You claimed it one way then, and another as the years have passed. From the moment I met you, heard that sweet sassy little voice, I have never been free. I have always been yours." He smiles. "The last few years have been a terrible, beautiful agony, but I would rather be with you, unable to show my love, than not be with you. And even though I know the two dates you went on were not what you would even call dates, I was so afraid you would one day start dating seriously and fall for someone."

"I understand. I worried that you would one day write me and announce your engagement. I've sometimes cried myself to sleep at night because I worried, and I needed to be with you." Turning in his arms, I slip mine around his neck and he holds me close. His sweet breath fans my lips and I am dizzy with longing.

His gaze delves into mine. "For four years, *cara mia*, I have longed to taste your kiss, to let you know the taste of mine."

"Then let me know it now," I breathe. "Please."

He doesn't hesitate. The first touch of his mouth against mine sends heat surging through me, and when his hands splay over my back, pressing my body flush against his, my legs weaken and it takes a great deal of effort to remain standing. His mouth is sweet, moist, heated, and experiencing his affections is the most perfect thing I have ever known or ever will know.

His mouth moves from mine, traveling to my neck and shoulder, and every inch of me cries out for him. I've never know such a feeling in all my life. I never knew it existed. When his lips are finally pressed against mine again, the muscles in his mouth work such a spell on me, I have to pull away for fear of passing out. Resting my forehead against his, I attempt to slow my breathing.

He takes my face in his hands. "Marry me, Dominique." The emotion I hear in his voice brings fresh tears to my eyes. "Please say you will be my wife." With gentle hands, he wipes my tears. I have dreamed of this for so long. I've imagined him saying these words to me a thousand times.

"I will," I manage to voice around the thick emotion in my throat. "It is all I have ever wanted."

He rewards me with his beautiful smile and kisses me again before reaching into his pocket and presenting me with a small yellow box. "Now you can have your present, and believe me, I searched long and hard for this box."

Grinning, I kiss him again, delighting in the fact that now I can kiss him any time I want. "It's beautiful."

"You haven't even seen what's inside."

"I know, but it's still beautiful because of the effort that went into finding it."

"I'm happy you are pleased," he says, opening the box.

On a velvet cushion rests a single one carat solitaire set on a platinum band. It's stunning and beautiful, coming in second only to him. Taking the ring from the box, he places it on my finger.

"Happy Birthday, sweet twenty-one."

Unable to reply, I draw his head down, meeting his mouth with mine, knowing this action will say more than mere words ever could.

Two weeks later

Wearing the yellow Greek goddess gown (because Marcello asked me to and it's definitely fitting) among the grove of olive trees on the Giannini land, Marcello and I exchange vows and rings, pledging to love, honor and cherish each other forever. Our wedding plans had been quick but neither of us could wait a day longer than necessary to marry. We've already waited long enough.

***

In the same grove, we lie in each other's arms, our energy spent from passion shared as we made love, our only witnesses being passing birds. Our parents have left for a week long vacation together in Greece, so we have the house to ourselves. And because of the memories this place holds for me, we can't think of a better way to start our honeymoon. We lazily gaze at one another.

"I can't believe you are really mine," he says, his loving gaze roaming over my face.

"I was about to say the same thing," I say with a smile. "But truthfully, I have always been yours."

"I have dreamed of this, you know?" he tells me. "For the last two years, each time I came back from visiting you, I walked through this grove for weeks afterward. I sat among the trees and dreamed of one day bringing you out here as my bride, and making passionate love to you. At times I felt like a lecherous old man, but I could not stop my heart from wanting you."

"Can I tell you something?" When he nods, I share my dream of the same event. "I used to dream of you making love to me in front of the family room fireplace." His eyes widen and I laugh. "Of course since this is your parent's place, I knew it was impossible and would never happen, but I still let my mind linger on it."

"Nothing is impossible, my sweet Domi." He brushes his thumb over my lips. "Do you have any idea of how much I love you?"

I snort and he chuckles. "I think I have some idea." I sober, pressing a hand against his handsome face. "Do you have any idea how glad I am that you loved me enough to wait thirteen years for me?"

"I think I have some idea," he repeats back.

He kisses me, smiling against my lips. "Now that I can truly love you, I don't think I will ever be near you without wanting to touch you, hold you, kiss you, and long to make love to you."

"Neither will I." I burrow into his chest, longing to be closer still. "I'm making up for lost time, or more for *your* lost time."

"I appreciate your concern." He lightly presses his mouth to mine, lingering a moment before his kiss travels over my jaw, moving to my ear. "Since we are making up for lost time, I think I'm ready to make love to you again," he whispers.

"I'm okay with that," is my breathless reply as his

warm mouth returns to mine and we again become lost in one another.

A moment later, thunder vibrates the world around us, bringing with it an instant downpour. We look at each other and laugh.

"This is fitting, don't you think?" Marcello asks as we jump up and wrap the blankets around us. Leaving our clothes where they are, we run up to the house. As soon as we enter, he sweeps me up in his arms and carries me to the family room, depositing me on the soft rug in front of the fireplace, then stretches out beside me.

"Now, my angel, where were we?"

A year later

Venice, Italy

Heaving a deep sigh, I lay on my back with my head resting in Marcello's lap. We have just finished our picnic lunch. My loving and attentive husband sits with his back against the balcony railing, caressing my seven-month-round stomach.

"Are you comfortable, *cara*?"

"I am, thank you." I pull a note pad and pen from the tote next to me. The pad is already half full with thoughts I've jotted down over the past year.

"What have you been writing, *amore*?"

"I've been writing about us, my love. About our love and how we came to be." I smile up at him. "It has all the makings of a great novel, don't you think?"

He laughs. "Yes, I would have to agree. What will you call this literary masterpiece of yours?"

"I'm not sure yet." I put the pad and pen down and raise up, draping an arm around his neck and pulling him closer. "I think I need a little more inspiration,"I say, kissing him.

Holding me, he says against my mouth. "I'm sure I can come up with something to help."

As I become lost in his blessed kiss and heated affections, he provides all the needed inspiration and more.

"How was that?" he asks, kissing my cheek.

"Mmm, that was a good start." I smile at the passion now burning in his gaze. "Maybe we should work on this inspiration thing some more."

"Whatever you say, baby girl," he says, jumping up and carrying me into the house.

About the Author

J. (Jewel) Adams stays crazy busy with her family and writing. She has written several books in different genres and is also a motivational speaker to both youth and adult audiences. She home schools her four kids that are still at home, and between that and conjuring up new ideas for her books, her brain is completely fried most of the time. She and her husband Sean are the parents of eight children, which means they are both losing hair, but hey, that's what Rogaine is for, right?

In her spare time (when she has any) she likes to curl up with a good book and a healthy stash of orange Tic Tacs. She and her family reside in Utah.

Jewel loves hearing from her fans, so if you would like to contact her to tell her how much you love her books or give her sympathy for the fried brain, or suggestions for the hair loss problem (for her husband, of course) contact her at jewela40@gmail.com

Website: **JewelAdams.com**

Blog: **jewelsbestgems.blogspot.com**

Other books by J. Adams/Jewel Adams
Still His Woman
The Legacy
The Wishing Hour
Tears of Heaven
Place In This World
The Journey
Against the Odds
Mercedes' Mountain
Guardian of My Heart

Ebooks
The Wishing Hour
The Legacy
Tears of Heaven
Place In This World: The Sequel to The Journey
The Journey
Mercedes' Mountain
That Kind of Love
The Shelter of His Arms
What the Heart Sees
The Sound of Love
Stories of the Heart
Against the Odds
Guardian of My Heart
Elise's Heart
For Love of Angel

Children's Book
Forbidden Portals: The Quicksilver Project

All Books Are Also Available in Kindle and Nook Versions (Elise's Heart and Mercedes' Mountain excluded)

Sweet 21 Birthday Ball